ONE
MORE
FLIGHT

ONE
MORE
FLIGHT

Eve Bunting

Illustrated by
Diane de Groat

A YEARLING BOOK

Published by
Dell Publishing Co., Inc.
1 Dag Hammarskjold Plaza
New York, New York 10017

Text Copyright © 1976 by Eve Bunting
Illustrations Copyright © 1976 by Diane de Groat

Yearling ® TM 913705, Dell Publishing Co., Inc.

ISBN: 0-440-46640-7

Reprinted by arrangement with Frederick Warne & Co., Inc.
Printed in the United States of America
Second Dell Printing– August 1979

CW

TO THE MEMORY OF MY PARENTS

Mae and Sloan Bolton

ONE
MORE
FLIGHT

1

Dobby scrambled up the scrubby hillside. Red dust rose in puffs around his tennis shoes, and his bare chest was a light red-brown color, smooth as spray paint. Dobby's breath came loud, and he felt the chokiness again in his throat. Time to stop and rest.

He untied the sleeves of the tan shirt he had knotted around his waist, wiped his sweaty hair, and retied the sleeves again. He'd come a long way. They would never find him now.

Darkness was closing in, and the October night would quickly get cold. Dobby felt a rush of fear when he thought of the night, but he swallowed it down and began walking toward the trees. The last time he ran away he hitched a ride and slept in a doorway downtown, right in the middle of Los Angeles. That was scary all right. All those old men wandering around hugging bottles. One of them wanted to share Dobby's doorway, but he kicked and yelled and the man went away. Of course that was last year when he was only ten. He didn't think he'd be so easy to scare now.

Maybe he could make himself a den up here, stay forever. He smiled. There he'd be, like some sort of jungle boy, eating berries, digging for roots and things. A tree house would be even better. He'd have a rope to swing himself up and down, and when his clothes wore away he'd go without any. There'd be nobody to see. And who cared anyway? It would be great. He'd just check the place out and see what he could find.

It was shadowy under the trees and he smelled the earth smell, old and damp and slightly rotten. He wondered how far back the trees went. Was he in a forest? The leaves whispered around him and above him and under his feet. He walked carefully through the trees. A bare hillside swept down below him, and Dobby saw that there was no one following him. There was no one but him in the whole empty world.

Something slithered across the dry brown earth.

Dobby jumped back. A snake? A rattler maybe? He stood behind a tree, his heart pounding, his mouth suddenly dry. He hadn't figured on snakes.

Maybe a tree house wasn't too smart an idea with snakes around.

The slithering came again, uneven, jerky, like paper crumpling. Dobby peered around the scabby tree trunk and saw something on the ground. It was something weird, pinkish white, without any shape as far as he could see. It moved across the ground in little hops. Dobby took a step forward. There was a string tied to it, a long string that stretched out of sight. The thing jerked again. It was a piece of raw chicken, and someone was trailing it. Why? Dobby scratched at a mosquito bite on his stomach and frowned. There *was* another person in the world.

A rush of air whirled past him. It was so sudden and fierce that his mind didn't notice until his eyes saw a big brown and white bird, the legs dangling below it like lifeless rubber, the wings jagged on the edges. There was a flash of dull pink as the tail feathers folded. The bird was on the ground, pulling the meat from the loop of string. It took the food whole into its sharp, curved beak, cramming it in with great gulps.

The wings opened again, and Dobby saw two deep-set eyes swivel toward him. The bird screamed once and rose, whipping the air, a mere two inches from Dobby's face as it veered toward a high branch and landed. Dobby let out his breath.

The bird sat motionless in the tree above him.

What was it? An eagle? He had never seen an eagle. A hawk? He wiped his sweaty hands along the sides of his jeans, and his stomach settled a little when he saw the bird's head turn away. The bird didn't care about him. It was waiting—waiting for something.

A tall figure stepped from the shadows. He had a leather harness across one shoulder, with a leather bag attached to it at the waist.

Dobby moved back, careful not to make any noise. He watched the man reel in the string and stash it in the pocket of his corduroy pants. On one hand he wore a bulky leather glove. As he came closer, Dobby saw that his hair was blond and shoulder-length. He was thinner than anybody Dobby had ever seen, and now Dobby saw that he wasn't a man, he was a boy, about eighteen. The tall boy looked up at the bird. He took something from the bag and held it up in his gloved hand, then whistled, high and clear, creating an echo in the trees like a train whistle in a long tunnel.

The bird screamed and poked its head forward. Dobby felt the draft as the bird dropped. Its talons curled around the boy's fist and the bird swallowed the meat that was held between the boy's gloved fingers.

Leaves crackled under Dobby's feet, and the blond boy looked up quickly and then down again. He fastened a loop of leather around the bird's legs

and Dobby saw a short length, like a dog's leash, dangling from the glove. The boy made soothing sounds, his uncovered hand stroking the bird's mottled breast feathers. He peered over at Dobby. Dobby waited.

Everyone always asked the same questions. "Who are you? What are you doing here? Why aren't you in school?"

But the boy said nothing. He stood, soothing and stroking the bird on his fist.

Slowly, Dobby stepped from the trees. "What kind of a bird is that?" He scratched mechanically at his mosquito bite.

"Red-tailed hawk."

Dobby came closer. "What's his name?"

"Corgo."

"What's that lump in his neck?"

"The chicken. He stores it there in his crop to eat later. He's not too hungry right now."

"Oh." Dobby took another step forward.

The boy pushed his hair back from his face with his free hand and began walking through the trees. Only the hawk turned its head to see if Dobby followed.

Dobby bit his lip. Darkness hung over the tops of the branches and a small night wind rustled the leaves. Being by himself, having a tree house, didn't sound so great any more. He undid the sleeves of his shirt and pulled it on.

"Hey," he yelled. "Wait up, will you?"

He had to run to overtake them. "Where are you going?"

"Home," the boy said.

The hawk suddenly squealed and flew a few inches above the glove, his wings thrashing wildly. The boy soothed him with a word and the touch of his hand.

Dobby wanted to say, "I don't have a home." That would get the boy's attention all right. But maybe it would be a dumb thing to do. He might start asking questions, or maybe begin thinking and guessing.

They came out of the stand of trees onto a dirt road that curved down the brown hillside, and Dobby saw a dusty green jeep with a dented fender.

The boy strode across the bare earth. Small rocks loosened under his feet and rattled down the slope. The last rays of the sun slanted through the night clouds, making the boy's shadow a thin shaft and the bird's shadow a monster blur on his arm. He opened the back of the jeep, undid the leather loop, and launched the hawk inside.

Dobby watched him climb behind the wheel. "Wait! Wait!" he called, running now, slipping and sliding down the hillside to get to the open window on the passenger side.

The boy's eyes reflected the dark blue of the work shirt he wore.

"Can I come with you?" Dobby asked.

"Why?"

"I've no place to go." There was a sort of whine in his voice and he added quickly, "My parents have gone away for the weekend. I could come with you . . . just till Monday."

The boy's stare was long and direct, and it made Dobby uneasy. He scuffed his feet in the dirt and kicked aimlessly at one of the worn tires. "There's no one to miss me, honest." He felt on surer ground here and tried to smile.

The boy nodded toward the empty seat beside him. "Well, get in," he said.

Dobby pulled open the door. Wow, he thought. Wow, that was easy.

The engine pulsed and the boy's hands were long and brown on the steering wheel. There were small white lines—scars—crisscrossing his wrists. He swung the jeep in a wide arc and changed gears. Then they were bumping down the path, following the wheel tracks that ran straight as rulers. And they were rattling away from the Residential Treatment Center. Away. Away. Dobby looked up and sideways. "I'm Dobby. Peter J. Dobson, but everyone calls me Dobby."

"Timmer."

The dirt road became a paved highway, and Dobby settled himself back against the smooth seat and watched the sun drop behind the low hills. Things seemed to be working out for once. For a second he allowed himself to remember the warnings at the Center about getting into cars with strange men. Well heck, this was a jeep. No one had said anything about jeeps. And Timmer wasn't a man. Kind of, but not exactly. Anyway, who cared about the Center's rules? He'd left forever.

"Do you live near here?"

"Pretty near."

"With your parents?" He hoped the parents wouldn't make a big hassle when Timmer arrived with a strange guy tagging along.

"Nope," Timmer said. "No parents. Just me, and Steve and Bob. And the birds of course. Right now it's just me and the birds."

"Oh." Dobby noticed how the wind whipped Timmer's long hair across his face and made the pointed collar of his workshirt flap wildly, like wings beating. Just him and the birds. Maybe it would be all right. His stomach jumped. It better be all right. There wasn't much he could do about it now.

2

Dobby sat up straight as Timmer pulled into the parking lot of a small market.

"I'll be back in a minute," Timmer said. "I have to pick up some things."

"Sure." Dobby slid down in the seat again. Might as well stay out of sight, just in case. Timmer had cut the motor and Dobby could hear the heavy movements of the hawk in the back. It was weird sitting there knowing the big old bird was just inches away behind his head.

He nibbled on his thumbnail. Maybe he should split, go now while he had the chance. They'd come a long way. If he was lucky he could lose himself somewhere and never be found. Dobby's hand was on the handle of the jeep door when Timmer came out of the market carrying a paper sack. He set it on the floor between them, and Dobby saw bread, a few cans, and a carton of milk.

"Hungry?" Timmer asked and Dobby nodded. "I'll fix us some chili." He switched on the jeep lights and their glare sliced the dusk, making the night around them darker, blacker than it was before.

Dobby chewed at the skin he'd loosened on the edge of his thumb. "How come you're . . . by yourself?" he asked.

"Steve and Bob—Bob's Steve's dog—they're up in Oregon. They'll be back pretty soon."

It sounded neat. Dobby imagined how it would be, living by yourself, doing what you wanted to do, getting up late, staying up as long as you liked. He sighed.

The road unrolled in front of the headlights. It was a country road with little frame houses set far apart and not too much traffic passing by.

"Are we still in the valley?" Dobby asked.

"Yep. Only eight miles from Glendon," Timmer said.

Dobby looked at him quickly. Glendon—where the Center was. Did he know? Had he guessed?

Timmer stared straight ahead. The fingers of his left hand tap-tapped on the steering wheel.

They passed a picket fence that ran along the road, and Dobby felt the pulse of the jeep slow. Timmer nosed the jeep into a narrow driveway. In the headlights Dobby saw a gate and the shine of a heavy lock and chain.

Timmer stopped and jumped out. He fumbled in his pocket for a key, unlocked the gate, and swung it open. When he had driven through, he locked up carefully behind them.

Dobby sat on the edge of the seat. The sound of the key turning made him jumpy.

The jeep poked up a long rutted lane. Old cars like rusted skeletons squatted in the dust. Ahead, a line of low hills shadowed the night sky.

Timmer swung around in front of a square unpainted barn and stopped. When he cut the headlights, the night rushed to surround them.

"You get the groceries, Dobby," he said. "I'll take Corgo." He opened the back of the jeep and a dim light went on inside.

Dobby held the sack while Timmer pulled on his glove and fixed the leather thongs to the hawk's legs. The soft short strips dangled down between his gloved thumb and finger, and Dobby saw how he held on to them.

"Is that Corgo's leash?" he asked.

"His jesses," Timmer said. "They make him easier to handle. Stay close behind me, Dobby. It's kind of dark around here."

It was darker than anything when he banged the jeep door closed.

Dobby followed him around the side of the barn, his eyes getting used to the shape of a path and the

23

shadowy outline of the building. The sky was a dusky color, not wholly black, and there was the beginning of a moon creeping over the far hills. A wide space behind the barn suggested an open field, but there was no softness of grass, and the dirt underfoot was dry and loose as sand. A gravel path bordered by shrubs cut through the middle, and it chewed at Dobby's toes, biting through his tennis shoes.

One of the shrubs moved, a head turned, a claw flexed. Dobby stopped and almost dropped the grocery bag. Birds! The shrubs were big birds, sitting on pedestals. A line of them stretched along the path into the darkness. They crouched silent as statues while Timmer placed Corgo on an empty pedestal. There was a light clink of metal as he tethered the hawk to the perch. Dobby swallowed. What kind of flipped-out place was this anyway?

Timmer pushed past him and jumped the three steps to the door at the back of the barn. "I'll get a lamp lit," he said.

Dobby held the groceries and waited. He should have split when he had the chance. He should never have come.

Timmer swung the door open. "Come on in." A match scraped, and light spilled from a Coleman lantern.

The barn was almost empty. Two sleeping bags were neatly rolled on rubber pads on the floor. There was a shelf that held a four-burner stove, another that held dishes, and another piled with books. There was a table, two wooden chairs, and a refrigerator, yellowed with age, that sat on fat claw feet. Wooden crates were stacked by a wall. Shadows filled the corners, and somewhere a clock ticked like water dripping into a tin.

Timmer set the lantern on the table.

A shuffling sound in the gloom made Dobby edge toward the circle of lamplight.

A brown bird, big as a turkey, fluttered on half-opened wings toward the table. Timmer bent over it. "How's it going fellow? How you doing?"

The bird had only one leg and he moved with a lopsided hop, one wing extended for balance.

"What happened to *him?*" Dobby asked. The spoken words made everything seem less weird. He held the sack of groceries tightly in front of him, like some kind of crazy lumpy shield.

"He's all messed up. I think a dog got him." Timmer took a piece of meat from his pouch and held it out. The bird grabbed and swallowed the meat in one gulp, and Dobby saw again the old white scars on Timmer's hands and understood— wounds from beaks or talons. He moved himself quietly behind a chair.

Timmer pulled off his harness and pouch. The leftover meat inside was in a plastic bag and he closed the bag tightly and put it into the refrigerator.

"Is he a hawk, too?" Dobby hoped Timmer

didn't notice the dumb way he was following him around.

"He's a Cooper's hawk, the kind farmers call a chicken hawk." Timmer took the grocery sack and began emptying it. The cartons of milk with the jersey cows grinning on their waxed fronts looked nice and ordinary. Timmer's voice was ordinary, too, and Dobby let his stomach relax. He had been holding himself so tight that he hurt.

"That seems kind of impossible. I mean, how did a dog get him? Couldn't the bird fly away?"

"This one didn't know any better," Timmer said. "Somebody probably stole him from the nest when he was a fledgling. His mother never had time to teach him anything." Timmer lifted the lantern and held it high.

The hawk squawked up at him.

"The somebody kept him in a cage for a couple of years till he got tired of him. Then he turned him loose. So the dumb thing doesn't know how to hunt for his own food, and he's starving to death. When he sees a man and his dog, he comes down begging and . . ." Timmer stamped with one foot on the wooden floor and both Dobby and the hawk jumped. Timmer grinned. He walked across the floor carrying the lantern. The big bird hopped after him, and Dobby saw that a corner of the barn was fenced off with chicken wire.

Timmer shooed the bird inside and closed the wire door. "I leave him free when I'm out," he said.

"He needs the exercise. But he's penned while I'm here."

"Is he dangerous?" Dobby asked.

"Sure," Timmer set the lamp on the shelf by the stove. "He's a wild creature. Would you like to sleep with a bobcat or a fox roaming the room? Same thing. That's what the someone discovered. A hawk's no cuddly pet. That's not the way he's made."

Timmer's long scarred hands worked at lighting the stove, opening cans, pouring milk into jelly glasses, setting two blue dishes and two spoons on the rickety table.

Dobby sat, staring around, making no move to help. From time to time Timmer glanced up at him, but they didn't talk any more, not even when the bowls were scraped clean and one of the milk cartons was empty.

"Good chili," Dobby said at last.

Timmer slid back his chair and nudged one of the sleeping bags with his toe. "You take this roll. I have a couple of things to do outside." He put the dirty dishes on a shelf. "We have a faucet out back. We'll scrub these off in the morning."

Dobby stood by the sleeping bag. "Is this your friend's?"

Timmer nodded. "Steve's."

"Does he help you with the birds?"

"Yeah."

Dobby burped gently. "Where do you get all

these hawks and birds, anyway? Do people give them to you?"

"Some do, when they get tired of caring for them. They call the Audubon Society and they call us. Or else the Humane Society gets them somehow and brings them here. It's against the law to have an eagle, and you need a falconer's license to keep a hawk, but that doesn't stop people trying to do it anyway. Sometimes we have so many birds out here we can hardly handle them."

Dobby felt a tick of excitement start somewhere deep inside him, and it spread and warmed till he could hardly stand it. "I bet there's lots to do," he said, keeping his voice casual. "I could hang around for a while and help if you like." He wished he'd offered to fix the chili.

Timmer didn't answer, and Dobby remembered the mother and father he'd made up, the ones who went away for the weekend. "My parents won't worry," he said. "I come and go all the time. Honest, they're used to me."

Timmer was lighting another lantern, taking his time about it, polishing the glass globe with the sleeve of his shirt.

"Well, what do you say?"

Timmer took something from one of the crates. Dobby couldn't see what it was, but it rattled when he pulled it out.

"I'm good at learning things," Dobby said. "I could learn about the birds." He stopped, trying to think what else to say. "I don't eat much." He remembered the third helping of chili and wished he hadn't accepted it.

"I have things to do outside," Timmer said again. "We'll talk when I get back." He stuffed the bundle from the crate under one arm and took the lantern. The door creaked shut behind him.

In the quiet of the barn Dobby heard the slow shuffle of the chicken hawk. There were other sounds, slidings and murmurings and sighings.

He took off his shoes and socks, his jeans and his shirt, and squirmed into the sleeping bag. It smelled of dog, a good raunchy smell. He guessed Steve's dog must have wriggled in beside him nights when they were both here.

Maybe if Timmer let him stay he could get a dog, too. He'd always wanted a dog, the kind that had little short legs and a belly that touched the ground. The kind with long ears that dangled so low the fool dog kept tripping over them. Of course, the birds might grow on you when you got to know them better. No telling.

It seemed a long time before he heard the creak of the big door and felt the barn brighten with the light from the extra lantern. He sat up. "Hey! I should have gone out and helped you. What were you doing anyway?"

"I had the owls to feed and the alarm to rig."

"Alarm?"

"Yeah! People try to steal our birds. It's great when Steve has his dog around. But when I'm alone I fix up a warning signal. There's been a pick-up truck driving slow out on the road. I've seen it two or three times this week." Timmer took off his clothes and padded across the wooden floor to one of the crates. Dobby saw him winding up an old beat-up alarm clock, the key creaking as he turned it.

"Why would anyone want to steal the birds?" Dobby wondered if Timmer was paranoid the way Joe Wheeler was at the Center, always thinking every other kid was trying to steal his washcloth. He'd had treatment, but the treatment hadn't helped any. Now Joe hid his soap, too.

Timmer blew out the two lamps. "There's always somebody who wants to be different. And to have a caged eagle or a hawk in your backyard, man, that's class! Till it gets to be too much of a hassle one way or another."

Dobby's eyes picked out the long humped length of Timmer under the sleeping bag. "I could be your night watchman! Just till Steve gets back?" He held his breath, waiting.

Timmer sighed. "You know the time I went into the market? I called Mrs. Pruitt down at the Center. I told her you were safe and I'd bring you back in the morning if that was O.K."

Dobby listened to the barn settling around them.

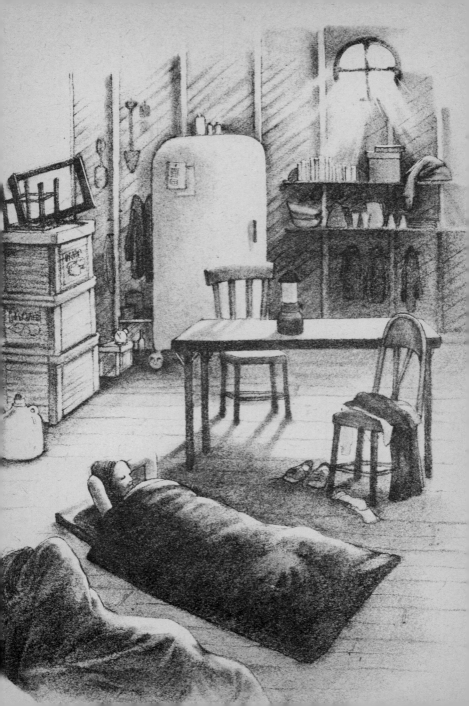

Weak moonlight sifted through a high dusty window. Cobwebs swayed gently like weeds under water.

"How did you guess?" he asked.

Timmer's voice was soft. "I don't know. A look maybe. I've lived in Glendon all my life. I went to school with the kids from the Center. They kept changing. But they all had the same kind of look—a reaching-out look."

"Yeah, well I'm reaching out all right. I'm glad you noticed." Dobby rolled over so his back was turned to the other sleeping bag.

"I might have known," he said. "Anybody who'd keep birds chained up—wild birds!" He felt tears smarting behind his eyes. "What's the difference keeping them chained and putting them in a cage? No use expecting you to understand what it's like in the Center or in those dumb foster homes."

"No, I guess not." Timmer's voice was sad. "There's nothing I can do about it, that's all."

"You don't understand and you don't care one bit."

Outside one of the birds squawked, loud and angry.

"Yeah, bird," Dobby said. "I hear you. I know how you feel."

He didn't answer when Timmer said good night.

3

Except for the short periods he had spent in five different foster homes, Dobby had always lived at the Center. He lay in the sleeping bag that smelled of dog and thought of all the times he'd run away before.

There were nine altogether, five times from foster homes and four times from the Center. But somehow he never got to stay away for long. Two days was the most so far. It was scary how hard it was just to keep from getting caught and sent back.

Dobby didn't know anything about his father. His mother had died when he was very young and he didn't remember her either. But he did remember his grandmother. The child-care worker in charge at the center, Mrs. Pruitt, told him his grandmother had loved him a lot. She didn't want to give him up, but she got too old and had to go to a place herself where people would look after her.

For a long time when he was little Dobby believed his grandmother would get out of her place somehow and come back and get him. He didn't want to go to any of the foster homes. What if Gran came looking for him at the Center and he wasn't there.

Come to think of it, that might have been why he ran away the first time from the Barclays. The memory was dim, but he didn't think they were too bad. Not like the Gravensteins with their goody-goody ways and little mean eyes.

After a while, he figured his Gran wasn't coming back. Like Karl Miller said, she probably decided the money she got from Dependent's Aid didn't make up for having to live with a creep like Dobby. Karl was older and knew everything.

Betsy Carstairs said his grandmother probably didn't like him because he lied so much. But Karl said nuts to that, grown-ups lied all the time themselves. Karl and Betsy came back to the Center a lot, too. They were still being treated for their problems.

Their social workers would have them in for private talks. Karl's was a guy named Daniel, and Karl said he was full of the same old stuff.

"What went wrong, Karl? Maybe we could talk about ways to make it better the next time . . ."

Sure was easy for Daniel to sit there and talk, Dobby thought. Daniel was all safe and sure of himself. Daniel wasn't a bit like them.

The funny thing was, Dobby had just about made up his mind that the next time they placed him with a family he'd try to stay. Then he discovered they weren't trying to place him any more. There was talk about finding out what motivated him to run away and stuff like that. He kept waiting to be called into Mrs. Pruitt's office for the usual jive. "You've made real good progress, Dobby. We think you're ready to go out with a family again." But the summons from Mrs. Pruitt never came. He'd even stopped lying except in emergencies in case old dumb Betsy was right.

Then three days ago old dumb Betsy had been placed with a neat-looking guy and his wife. The guy had a beard. Dobby cried in bed that night. Crying wasn't something he did too often. So why was he crying now, lying in this smelly old sleeping bag, looking up at the cruddy rafters?

He turned his head cautiously to look at Timmer. Timmer's long hair fanned across his face. There was a soft whishing sound every time he breathed out. You're just like everyone else, Dobby thought. I bet if I really had a mom and dad like I pretended, I bet if I hadn't been a crummy kid that nobody wants, I could have stayed. Probably think I'd steal your dumb birds or something. Dobby felt the hot stinging behind his eyes again and he sat up blinking hard, trying not to sniff. No use lying here feeling all sorry for himself. He'd have to go. And he would find somewhere else, somewhere better than this creepy old barn. He would look out for himself.

He edged gently out of the sleeping bag and got dressed. He would take one of the lanterns, leave it at the end of the driveway. His fingers found the lamp and the matches. He tried to walk lightly, but the old floor creaked and groaned with every step. The door creaked even more as he eased it open. He peered back at Timmer. The whishing sound kept up its slow, gentle rhythm. Timmer hadn't moved.

Outside it was brighter than inside, and Dobby saw that the moon had climbed high above the hills and that the sky was scattered with stars. The driveway that led to the road was darker, shadowed with thick oaks, and he was glad he had brought the lantern. He'd light it when he got far enough away.

The field lay clear in the moonlight and he saw the two lines of birds, stripped by the thin shade of the eucalyptus trees. For a minute he thought about setting them free, opening every one of the locks, shooing them off their perches and into the air.

Yeah! He closed his eyes and the night sky suddenly filled with beating wings, the air thick with

38

screams of freedom. It would serve Timmer right. He would come rushing out:

"Why, Dobby?" he'd ask. "Why did you do it?"

"All creatures should be free," Dobby would say.

Timmer would nod. "You're right, Dobby. Why didn't I see that before? Stay here with me, Dobby. We'll work together. Farm or something. Grow vegetables."

Dobby smiled in the dark, and he wished and he wished that that was the way it would be. But what if he freed the birds and they came after him instead of flying away into the darkness? He wouldn't put it past them. He sighed. It was funny how imagining made things better for a while and worse when you remembered how it really was. Far off on the road he heard a car or a truck. A mile away? Two? He'd better start moving.

He felt his way cautiously along the side of the barn and onto the driveway. Would someone pick him up and give him a ride? He shivered. Maybe he should have waited till it was closer to morning.

Here, under the oaks, the darkness swallowed him. He took a step, and another, and then suddenly his foot caught on a wire. There was a clashing, rattling noise that went on and on as he tried to get up to free himself from whatever it

was that was twined around his legs. The more he struggled, the noisier it got.

The barn door banged open, and from where he lay on the driveway he could see Timmer on the top step. He looked like a crazy giant as he came jumping down, a baseball bat swinging in his right hand.

"Timmer! Timmer! It's me." Dobby called.

Timmer stopped. "Dobby?" He came into the blackness under the trees as Dobby fumbled with the mess of string twisted around him. What in the world was it anyway?

"I'll get the lantern," Timmer said.

"There's one here somewhere. I dropped it." Dobby got matches out of his jeans pocket and struck one. In the wavering light he saw that he was tangled in a jumble of empty tin cans and old saucepan lids. A great bell was tied on the rope too. It was big as the bell on a fire truck.

Timmer found the lantern and Dobby lit it from another match.

"I told you about the alarm," Timmer said.

Dobby stood up and brushed at the dust that covered his jeans. He kept his face turned away from Timmer as they walked back to the barn. In silence he undressed and crawled into the sleeping bag. Timmer blew out the lamp. It was the way it had been before, only different.

"You were running away again," Timmer said.

Dobby nibbled at his nail.

"You're pretty good at running away, aren't you?" Timmer's voice was quiet.

Dobby didn't answer. No, he thought, I'm not good at it at all. If I was good at it I'd have gotten clear to Peru or somewhere by now. If you want to know, I'm rotten at running away.

The clock ticked and moon shadows flitted like bats among the moving cobwebs that clung to the roof. Maybe Timmer would go to sleep again and this time Dobby would know enough to step over the chain.

"Is it bad at the Center?" Timmer sounded wide awake.

"It's bad."

"Bad how?"

"You wouldn't understand." Dobby turned the hump of his back toward Timmer to show that the conversation was over.

"They give you enough to eat, don't they? Mrs. Pruitt's O.K.?"

Dobby sighed to show how stupid he thought Timmer was.

"We're not whipped if that's what you mean."

No use trying to explain to anyone on the outside that there were things that hurt just as bad as whipping. Things like having to go where they placed you and never belonging to anyone, not really anyway, and nobody caring about you because Karl Miller said families only took you for the money the state paid them, anyhow. But then, but then, look at the neat-looking ones old Betsy Carstairs got?

He thumped himself lower in the sleeping bag. Mrs. Pruitt was O.K. The time he had the measles she went out and bought him a *MAD* magazine and a dune buggy model with a top that clicked on and off. But still, she was usually too busy to talk or to listen.

And there were rules pinned on the walls, a time for lights out at night, and you had to sit inside and watch the people go by on the sidewalk. It felt like being in prison even though the Center was "an open setting" with no locks on the door. *No use* trying to explain to Timmer about the people and not being able to go out by yourself, ever, without permission, and . . .

"It's just . . . I'm not free!" He hadn't meant to say it so loudly, but that's the way the words came out, bouncing like balls off the rafters, making the Cooper's hawk flap wildly and shriek. Dobby felt the lump in his throat again and swallowed it down. He was getting to be like Mrs. Goddart, the cook at the Center, who cried all the time and told them it was because she was getting old. Maybe he was getting old, too. His teeth found his thumbnail and gnawed hungrily.

"Do you *know* why you always get brought back?" Timmer asked quietly.

"Sure," Dobby said. "People turn me in."

Timmer looked at Dobby for a long moment.

"Tomorrow would you like to stay with me, Dobby? I'm taking two of the birds up into the mountains to release them. You could come. I'll call Mrs. Pruitt in the morning and ask her if it's all right to bring you back Sunday instead."

Dobby heard the slow, steady beating of his heart. This was the first time ever that anyone invited him to stay with them. He turned the words around and around in his mind, searching for Timmer's reasons, wondering why Timmer wanted him to stay.

"What do you say, Dobby?"

"Sure, that would be O.K." He was proud of how cool his voice was. "Why are you releasing the birds anyway?"

There was the whispering sound as Timmer moved in his sleeping bag. "It's time for them to go," he said. "They're ready."

Dobby lay watching a small gray mouse high in the rafters polishing its nose with its front paws. A lizard moved silently up the wall. In the corner the hawk stirred.

Dobby rubbed his mosquito bite. He'd be here tomorrow night, and wouldn't it be something if Timmer changed his mind and let him stay forever?

He closed his eyes. Timmer would go striding into the hall at the Center. He'd be wearing his

44

blue work shirt and the old corduroys. Corgo would be on his arm and Timmer's big boots would leave red mud marks on Mrs. Pruitt's polished floor.

"I'm not bringing Peter J. Dobson back here," Timmer would say, and his voice would ring through the banisters, his eyes buggy with surprise and envy.

"I want all his things," Timmer would say. "And you can bet this boy'll never be back. Never! He's going to the best foster home you guys ever saw."

Dobby smiled. Wouldn't that be fantastic! He could hardly wait.

4

There was a bell ringing. It must be the wake-up bell, but it sounded different . . .

Dobby opened his eyes and remembered. Light sifted into the barn, and the window that had let in the moonlight was now an oblong of brightness high on the wall. The Cooper's hawk sat like a bundle of old feathers in its corner. The bell rang and rang.

Timmer padded barefooted across the floor, grabbed the clock, and gave it a bad-tempered swipe. The ringing stopped.

Dobby watched Timmer yawn and scratch his belly. He was skinny as a green bean, and when he stretched Dobby could count every one of the ribs that striped his chest. Dobby smiled.

He remembered how it had been in his mind when Timmer marched into the hallway at the center. The good sound of his voice ringing through the building.

But it wasn't true. It was just something else he imagined—one of those inside-his-head wishes that turned into lies if you didn't keep an eye on them. Timmer was going to let him stay for one day, then he was turning him back. Just like everyone did. Maybe he should try being nice to Timmer. Prissy old Betsy Carstairs always said that nice got you farther than nasty, and Dobby had to admit she'd gotten a lot farther than he ever had.

Timmer was rolling up his sleeping bag, placing it neatly at the bottom of the rubber pad. Dobby crawled out of his, too, fixing it exactly like Timmer's. He tried to be really with it, so Timmer would see how good it was to have Dobby in the mornings. "What do we do now?" he asked cheerfully, shivering, and wishing Timmer would make a move toward his clothes. It was cold in the barn. Drafts of air blew through the cracks in the wood, cold as currents in the ocean.

"Shower," Timmer said.

Dobby looked around. "Shower?"

"The faucet outside." Timmer pulled two towels off a hook on the wall and threw one at Dobby.

"Oh, sure," Dobby said. "The faucet." He shivered again.

Timmer opened the big door and took a deep

breath. It was a misty morning with water beading the trees and the thick hedges. In the dirt field the birds sat motionless on their perches, heads sunk low into their breast feathers, their long leather jesses slack around their feet. Now that it was light, Dobby could see that they were all big birds, and that there were maybe twenty of them, ten on either side of the path. Two, larger than the rest, were on perches under an oak tree, away from the others. He thought he recognized Corgo, but he wasn't sure. Rubber wading pools filled with water were scattered around the field. To one side were wooden huts with wire-mesh walls, and he could see bird shapes inside.

Timmer followed his glance. "The owls," he said. "I've got four right now. They like to be in the dark." He gave a soft whistle and got a screech in return. "That's Who," Timmer said. "He's a Great Horned Owl. Some dumb advertising guy used him in a cigar commercial. He kept him chained on a perch. You can't do that to an owl. Poor old Who got sores on his legs and he didn't look too pretty on camera. Now we've got him." He turned on a faucet and water flowed from the nozzle of a snaky green hose. "You want to go first, Dobby?"

The stream of water spilled over Dobby's shoulders, making him gasp and splutter and hop around in a kind of crazy dance. He threw the water over himself, scrubbing at his chest and shoulders, seeing yesterday's dust run off him in brown trickles and mix with the dust under his feet. There was something nice about that. The water was pins-and-needles cold.

"I'm clean, I'm clean," he yelled, and Timmer turned the hose from Dobby to himself, letting it run into his mouth, spouting it out again, whooshing and whomping, holding his thumb half over the nozzle to make a jet across his stomach.

"O.K.," he said at last, turning off the water and coiling the hose neatly before he dried himself off. "Let's eat."

Dobby sat at the table opposite Timmer and ate cereal from a pottery bowl. The cereal had raisins in it and nuts and little pieces of cut-up dates and apples, and Timmer had divided all the remaining milk between them so that the milk came almost to the rim of his bowl. It didn't taste like the corn flakes at the Center. Dobby tried not to make a slurping sound as he ate. See my good manners, Timmer? See what a nice polite kid I am?

He leaned back and closed his eyes. He and Timmer would be here, and the dog, too, the one with the long ears, and . . .

"Do your eyes hurt you, Dobby?"

Dobby sat up and blinked. He felt his face getting warm. "Naw," he said. "Sometimes I just . . . think better with them shut."

Timmer smiled. "I used to do that, too. I'd pretend I was Tarzan or Superman or somebody. You ever pretend that?"

"Sometimes." Dobby could hardly believe it.

Timmer tipped his head back and held the empty milk carton over his open mouth to get the last drop. Manners didn't matter all that much around here, Dobby decided. He found his mosquito bite with his fingers and scratched it happily.

"School was such a drag a lot of the time," Timmer said, "but I had to be there. So I'd just cop out inside my head. Sort of like running away from it all. Then one day I figured, what the heck. Wise up. If you open your eyes and look straight at things they're not so bad after all." He grinned again. "Not even school." He pushed back his chair. "We'd better get moving. Miss Bee will be here in a minute."

"Miss Bee?" Dobby couldn't get over Timmer's imagining just the way he did. Maybe all kids did. And how would you know anyway? "Who's Miss Bee?"

"She lives in the next house up the road. This is her land and her barn. She donates them and time, too, when I need it."

"How come?"

"She's a member of the Audubon Society. She knew we needed a place." Timmer rose.

"If you'll scrub off the dishes, I'll get the food ready for the birds."

Dobby carried the bowls from breakfast and the

ones from dinner outside and washed them carefully. He didn't know what to dry them with, so he
used one of the towels and finished them off by
rubbing them against his shirt.

He hoped Timmer would notice what a fantastic
job he did, but Timmer didn't even look up from
what he was doing. He was chopping meat into big
chunks on the top of a packing crate.

Dobby watched silently. His stomach heaved
and he took a deep breath. The deep breath was a
mistake. Right now the barn didn't smell too good.

"What . . . what kind of meat *is* that?" he
asked.

"Oh, everything. A mixture." Timmer went on
chopping. "We take whatever we can get."

Dobby swallowed. "Don't you . . . peel the fur
off first? I mean, *skin* it or something?"

"Nope," Timmer said. He dropped the chunks of
rabbit and squirrel and rat into a plastic bucket
by his feet. "The birds need all of it to keep their
crops and their stomachs clean. The bones, the fur,
everything. That's the way they eat in the wild.
People who keep them for pets don't understand
that. Then they wonder why the birds get rickets."

"Oh. Where do you get them? The . . . the . . ."
He struggled to find the least gross way to put it.
"The dead things."

Timmer wiped off the cleaver and the top of the
crate with a wet cloth. He rubbed blood from his
hands. "They're mostly road kills," he said. "I go

out in the jeep two or three mornings a week and pick up anything that got clobbered by the cars and trucks during the night. On these roads I find plenty. Then sometimes I take one of the birds out, and he'll make his own kill. What he doesn't eat I bring home to share with the others. When I'm really stuck, the Audubon Society gives me food money and I buy chicken in the market."

Dobby nodded. The Audubons, whoever they were, must be pretty nice to give away money and land and everything. Dumb, too, maybe.

Timmer carried the bucket, and Dobby followed him through the door into the morning.

The day was brightening and the mist had lifted from the tree tops. The birds wakened at their coming, stretching their wings over their heads like old men coming out of sleep. They squawked lazily, preening their breast feathers, watching Timmer and Dobby through half-closed eyes.

Timmer pulled on his glove and walked along the path, holding the pieces of meat between finger and thumb, going up one side of the path and down the other.

"Easy pickings today," he told the birds. "Tomorrow you have to work for it again. You're not here to be pampered and spoiled."

The two huge birds on the perches under the oak waited their turn.

"What are those?" Dobby asked.

"Golden eagles." Timmer pointed to the smaller

one. "She's going with us this morning." He pulled on a different glove before he fed the eagles, one that covered his hand and stretched all the way to his shoulder.

The smaller eagle fluttered off the perch to the ground. His wingspan was wider than Dobby was tall; her neck feathers looked like polished copper. "How do you know it's time to release her?" Dobby asked.

"I've taught her all I can. How to hunt for herself, how to be fast and fierce and wild again. I've helped her strengthen her wings. She's never been free to fly, so she didn't know how to use them. I can't do any more. It's up to her now."

Dobby nibbled at his thumbnail. Something edged at his mind, needled him, brought back a memory that disappeared before he could put a shape to it. "What if you're wrong?" he asked. "Suppose she's not ready to go? What'll happen then?"

Timmer scratched the eagle on the top of her head, and she pushed herself against him the way a dog does when it wants its back rubbed. "She'll die," he said. "If she's not ready she won't make it." He took the leather jess that tethered the eagle into his gloved hand, unhooked the swivel metal ring from her legs, and whistled her up onto his gloved fist.

Dobby stepped back. The eagle was so big and so scary. How could Timmer hold that weight on his arm? He must be real strong, stronger than he looked.

Timmer coaxed the bird onto the platform of a pair of scales, checked her weight, and fed her more meat.

"Just in case," he said. "She can carry enough food to keep her alive for four or five days. That'll give her a breathing space."

Dobby saw the huge chunks of meat in the eagle's crop, and he tried not to think what they were. Squirrel? Rat? "That's pretty neat," he said brightly. "Like taking a picnic."

Timmer grinned. His leather glove examined the eagle's beak. "I'm going to have to cope her before we go," he said.

Dobby nodded. "Yeah." Cope her? Better not ask dumb questions.

Timmer put the eagle back on the perch, weighed one of the red-tailed hawks, and fed it extra food, too. He washed the bucket under the faucet and rinsed off his hands.

"Are you going to cope with the eagle now?" Dobby asked. He hoped he sounded real interested.

Timmer laughed. "Not cope with. Just cope."

He went into the barn and came back with a short sharp knife and a small piece of black cloth. The eagle allowed him to put the hood over her eyes and to hold her beak in his gloved hand. Carefully, Timmer honed the beak, shortening it about a half inch.

Dobby leaned forward to see better. "It is kind of interesting, no kidding," he said absently, and saw Timmer's quick grin. He had the strangest feeling that Timmer knew all about him, how he was thinking and scheming and everything.

"They do their own coping in the wild," Timmer said, "on trees and roots and bones. This'll do her for a few months." He took the hood from the bird's head. "By then you'll be able to look after yourself, won't you, Happy?"

Dobby frowned. "Can a bird find its way back? I mean, suppose . . ." He stopped.

Someone was coming up the long dirt driveway from the road.

"It's Miss Bee," Timmer said, and he smiled.

Dobby watched the figure tramping purposefully toward them. If Timmer hadn't told him it was Miss Bee he never would have guessed.

She was small as Dobby and as thin. She wore baggy old jeans, the turn-up on the bottoms so wide they were folded almost to her knees. Her shirt was red-checked flannel and her boots yellow leather. As she got closer Dobby saw that her hair was white and cut so short that it stuck up all over her head in little tufts. Under her arm she carried a big white rooster, and in her other hand she waved an envelope. A whistle hung on a string around her neck. She stepped carefully over the alarm rope, lifting her leg so daintily that not one can jangled.

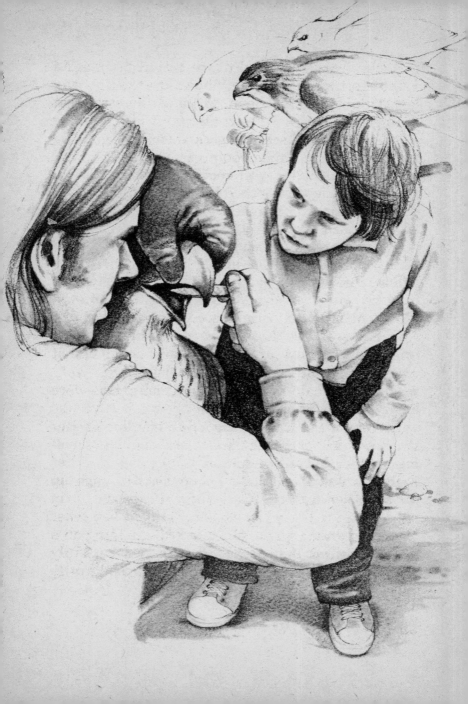

At first Dobby tried not to stare, but then he decided it didn't matter if he did or not. She was staring at him as if he were the one who looked strange, staring and pointing, too.

"Who's that?" Her head jerked from side to side like a chicken's, and Dobby expected to hear her start clucking. The rooster's head moved, too. His round yellow eyes watched Dobby carefully.

Dobby stepped back.

"This is Dobby, a friend of mine," Timmer said, and the words echoed and echoed like a small gong inside Dobby's head. A friend of mine. A friend of mine.

"Oh." Miss Bee thrust an envelope at Timmer. "You got a letter from Steve. Came yesterday." Her little hand found the rooster's head and stroked it gently, and Dobby saw the glint of about six big diamond rings on her fingers. "Well, when's Steve coming back?" she demanded. "Me and Rooster's been missing him."

Timmer stuck the coping knife in his belt and the hood in his pocket. He ripped open the envelope and pulled out the letter.

Dobby watched Timmer's face. Dobby imagined the words on the paper:

"Dear Timmer,
Bob and me have decided not to come back. Maybe you should get yourself another partner to work with the birds. Why don't you get someone

*young and train him? Somebody around eleven
would probably work out good. You'll need a new
dog, too. I've heard that the kind of dog that has
long floppy ears and short legs is especially good
for bird guarding. They hear well with those big
ears, and the short legs let them get right down
to where the smells are.*

*Your friend and ex-partner,
Steve"*

Silently Timmer finished the real letter, folded
it, and put it back in the envelope.

"Well?" Miss Bee asked.

"He's coming back tomorrow," Timmer said.

Miss Bee nodded and the rooster nodded, too.
Dobby felt the same kind of sickness he felt ear-
lier when he smelled the dead squirrels. So what
had he expected? Sure Steve was coming back.
He pushed his hands deep in his jeans pockets
and whistled soundlessly to show it didn't matter
a Jack Diddley to him.

"Good thing," Miss Bee said. "Lookee here."
She fished in the pocket of her jeans and pulled
out a handful of old cigarette ends. "Found them
down under the pepper trees by the road. Tire
tracks, too. Someone's been sitting down there,
watching the place. He's after the birds." The
rooster squawked nervously and Miss Bee
smoothed his feathers. "Not you, pet. Miss Bee
won't let anyone touch you."

Timmer took the cigarette ends and rubbed them between his fingers. "He was either there a long time, or there's more than one of him," he said. "You sure you can take care of things today, Miss Bee?"

"Sure I'm sure." She touched the whistle that hung around her neck. "Just let somebody try something. I'll blast him to kingdom come. Me, and Rooster, and this here whistle, and the baseball . . ." She stopped.

"Look out!" Timmer said. He held up one arm, pretending to duck. "You're one scary lady all right. But keep Rooster away from my hawks and the eagle or you know what'll happen."

Rooster screeched.

"Rooster knows," Miss Bee said, and Timmer grinned.

"That alarm's not much good in the daylight," Timmer said. "All someone would have to do is step over it. Just take it off, Dobby. It's better kept secret for nighttime."

Dobby released the alarm from the bushes while Timmer carried out the golden eagle and the red-tailed hawk and put them in the back of the jeep.

Dobby put the signal rope away inside. When he came back, Timmer was behind the wheel and he climbed in beside him.

"Good-bye," Miss Bee shouted, and she waved as they jolted down the driveway.

Dobby closed his eyes. Tomorrow night Steve'll be in the sleeping bag, and Bob'll be snuggled up next to him, and the Cooper's hawk will be in the corner, and the lizard, and the mouse, and Timmer . . . The lump in his throat felt as big as the lump in the eagle's crop, and telling himself he didn't care made no difference. There must be some way. What if he told Timmer what was going to happen to him?

He remembered the last time he was brought back. The meeting in Mrs. Pruitt's office. Miss Jackson, his social worker, was there, and two men, both of them uptight in dark suits and glasses. Dobby's heart pounded so hard he didn't catch their names or much of what they said. One thing he did hear, though.

"We can't have a boy at the Center who runs away all the time. It's bad for the other children." The one in the striped tie stood up.

"I'm sorry to have to tell you this, Peter," the man said. "Miss Jackson knows and we feel you should know, too. One more time and the Center won't take you back. You're gone more than you're here. It's foolish paying out money for a boy who's getting no benefits from what we're doing. Next time you'll have to go to Juvenile Hall."

Dobby had looked up into Mrs. Pruitt's face and her eyes were soft and misty, and Dobby couldn't stand it, couldn't stand any of it. He ran from the room without a word, banging the door against the silence behind him.

Juvenile Hall. It sounded terrible. It sounded like the worst place in the world.

Karl Miller said it was the worst place in the world. "Man, you'll never get away from there," he said. "Al Capone himself couldn't break out of Juvie." Karl was very up on the old-time gangsters. He had books about them.

Dobby had decided right then that he'd never run away again. The Center wasn't so bad. Some of the foster homes were probably O.K., too. He'd try harder. Juvenile Hall! But then, well, then dumb old Betsy was placed. When she left, the walls began to get tight again, and he hadn't meant to go, but he had. And now, here he was, and he couldn't find the words, the right words so that Timmer would let him stay.

Little houses slipped by them, and eucalyptus trees, and scraggy black hedges. They passed a grove of orange trees, the fruit round and golden, glowing like small lanterns among the shiny dark green of the leaves. One more time, he'd try. One more time. He sighed, and Timmer looked quickly across at him and then back to the road.

"Timmer, please, can I stay with you and Steve and Bob?"

Now, Timmer would say, "Yes, Dobby, I can see we need someone like you to . . ."

"No," Timmer said. "There's no way, Dobby. They wouldn't let us keep you. Have you any idea what people go through to be foster parents? The interviews and the questions and inspections. Anyway, I'm nineteen, Steve's eighteen, and I think Bob just turned three." He punched Dobby on the arm. "Come on, Dobby. You know I can't."

"I could hide. If they came you could say I'd run away, and then I'd come back and . . ."

"Can't do it, Dobby."

Dobby sat up straight. "Well, O.K. then," he said loudly. "You can bet your Jack Bull Diddley I won't ask you again."

"Dobby . . ."

"Don't talk to me. Just don't talk to me, O.K.?" Dobby moved himself as far away from Timmer as he could get. Telling Miss Bee he was Dobby's friend! Liar, Dobby thought. Liar, liar, liar.

5

Timmer swung the jeep into a service station and had it filled with gas. After he paid the fat attendant, he opened the door and turned toward Dobby.

"I'm going to call Mrs. Pruitt now," he said, "to see if it's O.K. to keep you another day. I'll be as fast as I can."

Dobby saw a phone box by the side of the station, the sun glinting off the smudgy, dusty glass walls. "What are you calling her for?" he asked. "Why don't you just take me back now? What's the difference? She won't let me stay, and I don't want to see your dumb birds set free anyway."

Timmer ran a hand through his hair. "You don't want to?"

"No." Dobby hunched his shoulders and let his chin rest on his chest.

"I'm sorry about that, Dobby. I'd better talk to her anyway and let her know you're all right." He was halfway across the concrete when Dobby opened the door and called, "O.K. I'll go with you."

Timmer smiled and waved. "Good!"

Dobby watched him leaf through the phone book and put money in the slots. Now he was talking, waiting, talking again.

What if Mrs. Pruitt did say no, Dobby can't stay another day; bring him back now, right away. What if Timmer said O.K. Boy, I can't take his bad temper any more anyway. You can have him.

He slunk low in the seat and licked his hangnail. It was raw on the edge and stung when the spit touched it. He dried it carefully on his shirt.

The sun twinkled on the keys where they dangled in the ignition. Dobby leaned across and nudged them with his fingertip, making them sway gently. Suppose he stole the jeep and drove away and never stopped till he got to China? He closed his eyes and smiled.

He'd be zipping along, the wheels whizzing, his hands strong and bony, like Timmer's on the wheel, a map spread on the seat beside him.

Zoom . . . *through a town.*

Wheee . . . *past every car on the road. His nose*

twitched to the smell of rubber burning. Look out, guys, here I come.

He opened his eyes and blinked. He was still here. Sure he was still here. He didn't know how to drive.

Timmer was frowning into the telephone, waving his hands as if Mrs. Pruitt had X-ray eyes and could see them all the way from Glendon. Why was he frowning? She *was* saying no, that's why. Timmer edged the door open with his foot, kicking it wide while he talked, stretching one long leg out into the sunlight.

Yeah, Dobby thought. You don't like to be cooped up either, do you, Timmer? You don't like it for five minutes, but you can't figure out why I don't want it for the rest of my life. It was suddenly hard for him to breathe and his chest felt like he had run too far too fast. He sat up and slid across to Timmer's seat.

You let off the brake, and then you move the gear around to make sure it's in neutral, and then you push in the pedal and turn the key.

The motor caught and Dobby pushed the gear lever forward. The jeep jumped, jumped again, and stopped. From the back the birds shrieked and scrabbled. He got a quick glimpse of Timmer's startled face.

"Hey!" Timmer's voice was almost drowned in

the engine sound as Dobby turned the key again. He saw Timmer leap from the phone box as the jeep hurtled forward and jolted to a stop. Timmer was coming. Dobby pushed in the clutch, pulled at the gear lever, and there was no sound now but the jeep rolling, rolling down the incline. There was no sound at all, not even from the birds. Someone had turned all the noise off as if it were a dream.

"The hand brake, Dobby! The brake pedal!"

Timmer shouting, and Dobby's hand finding the split prong that was the emergency brake, and his foot reaching for the floor and something coming fast, very fast, a pole with a sign that had words in big red letters.

It wasn't much of a crash, but it threw him forward against the steering wheel. Then Timmer had the door open and he pulled Dobby out, peering down into Dobby's face. The fat gas station man was there, too, and they made Dobby sit on the smooth, shiny concrete.

"How did it happen?" the gas man asked. When Timmer didn't answer, he wiped his hands on a greasy rag and glared at Dobby. "Foolin' around behind the wheel, were you?" He shook his head at Timmer. "And you hadn't no more sense than to leave the keys where he could get at them."

"No. I hadn't no more sense," Timmer said.

Dobby looked up.

"I'd like to kick the pants off you," Timmer said.

There was a tightness around his mouth and his eyes were tight, too.

Dobby watched Timmer walk to the back of the jeep and open the doors. His voice was soft as he spoke to the two birds, soft and soothing. Then he circled to the front and examined the smashed fender.

"He busted it good," the gas station man said with satisfaction, and Dobby wanted to smear the oil rag over his fat face.

"It'll match the busted one on the other side," Timmer said shortly.

"And look at my sign!"

"Yeah." Timmer took a crumpled wallet from the back pocket of his corduroys and pulled out a card. "I'll check if my insurance covers it."

"Won't cover with him driving." The attendant jerked a black-rimmed thumb at Dobby. He made a big production of taking down Timmer's address and the jeep's license number. And all the time Dobby sat on the bald cement that was warm and smooth as an eggshell, right out there in the open with no place to hide from the look on Timmer's face and the strange cold sound of Timmer's voice. He untied his shoelaces and tied them again to give himself something to do.

"Get in the jeep," Timmer said.

"I'm sorry about the fender."

"Get in the jeep."

Dobby climbed in and huddled in the seat while Timmer reversed and swung around the gas pumps. The sign teeter-tottered behind them but decided not to fall. Dobby blew on his fingers and examined his nail.

"I've really messed this thing up," he said. "You don't have a bandage, do you?"

Timmer didn't answer. The air from the open window streamed his hair out behind him.

"I thought probably Mrs. Pruitt wouldn't let . . ."

"You thought. But you couldn't wait to find out. You don't give anybody much of a chance, do you? You could have killed yourself, you know. *That* would have been real great!"

He leaned forward and switched on the jeep radio, turning the knob so music blasted like hot air around them.

Dobby looked miserably out the window. "You could have killed yourself, you know." Timmer's words circled in his mind and he knew he'd heard those words before, or words like them.

Jimmie Francis, the dumb little kid at the Center. He was gone now. Gone a long time ago. But they were on a Christmas outing once, and Jimmie pulled away from Mrs. Pruitt and ran across the street in front of a bus. The bus had missed him, but Mrs. Pruitt was furious, and she spanked Jimmie right there on the sidewalk. "You could have been killed!" she'd said, her words rising and falling with her hand. Her face was as red as the Santa Claus suit the fat guy wore in the department store.

Dobby had wondered why she was so mad anyway. Jimmie was so little, and dumb at that. Betsy Carstairs said it was because Mrs. Pruitt had been scared, that she cared a whole lot for Jimmie and she'd thought Jimmie was dead for sure. She'd get over being mad pretty quick, Betsy Carstairs said. And as usual, rotten old Betsy Carstairs was right. Mrs. Pruitt ended up hugging Jimmie and buying him a double-scoop ice-cream cone from Jiffy Freeze.

Dobby looked up and sideways at the thin brown face. Wow, he thought. Wow. He coughed softly, hoping Timmer would look at him, but the cough was drowned in the music.

"What *did* Mrs. Pruitt say anyway?" he shouted.

"I'm to take you back tomorrow before eleven."

"Oh." Probably another meeting at eleven with the guys in the creepy black suits.

"O.K., Peter Dobson. We hear you ran away again. Get your things packed. We'll take you to Juvie right now."

He traced the outline on his shirt where the pocket had been. A small thread clung and he pulled it out carefully. But not today. He didn't have to go back today.

74

He leaned forward, shouting so Timmer could hear.

"I know you're mad at me, Timmer, but . . ."

Timmer looked straight ahead. "You're wrong," he said. "I don't like getting my jeep smashed up, but I'm not mad anymore."

Dobby made a capital D with the thread on the knee of his jeans. He could hear in Timmer's voice that he wasn't mad. He was disappointed, disappointed in Dobby, and that was much worse. Even Betsy Carstairs couldn't find any good in that. He crumpled the D into a ball and dropped it on the floor.

Some goony guy on the radio was singing. The words filled the jeep, reaching down to touch a soft, secret place inside of Dobby, a place where it hurt.

Sometimes I feel like a leaf in the wind,
A leaf from a weeping tree.
And I cry and I cry to the wild, lonely wind,
Won't anyone listen to me?

6

They drove under a sky that was a soft cloudless blue, climbing higher and higher on the narrow country road. Pumpkins sat in fields, ripe and ready for Halloween markets. Wooden stalls by the roadside advertised fresh corn and tomatoes.

Around noon Timmer stopped again and bought four apples, newly picked, and tossed two of them on the seat beside Dobby. About an hour later he swung the jeep onto a dirt road that wound toward a horizon of craggy brown mountains and pine trees.

They climbed slowly, and Timmer didn't stop until the road ended. They sat for several minutes, the silence broken only by the tick, tick of the cooling engine. All around there was a Christmas-tree smell, and the air felt so good and so clear it made your head feel hollow inside just to breathe it.

Dobby sneezed, and the eagle in the back gave a *kee-yelp* of fright.

Timmer climbed out and sprawled on the warm hood of the jeep, and after a few minutes Dobby shrugged and followed him.

Below, the world fell away into a rocky brownness except for an occasional lush green orange grove or an apple orchard. It was so peaceful that Dobby felt a calmness spreading inside of him. He wished he hadn't done that dumb thing with the jeep. Today could have been a good day. Maybe even the best day of his whole life.

After a long time Timmer stretched and slid down from the hood. "I guess the birds would like to get out, too," he said. "We'll release the eagle first."

Dobby jumped down beside him. He touched the bent fender, rubbing the place where the metal showed through the green paint, wishing he could magically turn it back the way it was before. He watched Timmer ease his arm into the shoulder-length glove and take the jesses from the seat. Timmer hesitated for a second then abruptly pulled the keys from the ignition and put them in his pocket.

Dobby opened his mouth to protest, to say that no way would he try anything like that again, to ask what the Jack Diddley Timmer thought he

was. Didn't he trust him or something? But he didn't say anything. Like the dent in the fender, there was no magic way to rub out what he had done. He hurried ahead of Timmer to open the back door of the jeep.

The eagle flew at once to Timmer's fist as though she knew he had come for her, and in a few seconds the jesses were looped securely.

Dobby had to scramble to keep up as Timmer strode over the brown earth, Happy on his fist.

"Why did we bring them so far?" Dobby asked, unbuttoning his shirt and tying it by the sleeves around his waist the way he always did. He hated himself for his sucky-up voice that sounded just like old Betsy Carstairs', and he scowled. "Couldn't you have freed them back at the barn?"

"Huh-uh!" Timmer shook his head. "Too close to people down there."

He stopped and slid the jesses from Happy's legs. She sat motionless on his fist, her dark eyes watching him intently. Her crop was fat and round as though she'd swallowed a baseball.

Abruptly Timmer raised his arm, launching her into the air. She flapped close to the ground, awkward looking, the jagged edges of her wings seeming to sweep the dirt as she bumbled across it. Then she rose and settled on a round bare rock, her talons finding their own grip where Dobby could see no roughness or ridge.

80

Timmer stood very still.

Dobby resisted the urge to scratch the mosquito bite on his stomach. It had begun to itch again as soon as the sun had found it.

Happy crouched on the rock, her head poked forward, her golden hackles raised, her great wings hunched like shoulder blades.

For a long time she crouched, and Dobby blinked his eyes against the sunlight and waited with Timmer.

She began to call loudly, *"Kleap, kleap, kleap."* Suddenly she rose on partly flexed wings, and then, seeming to sense the open spaces beyond, she rose clear of the trees, rising hard-winged, black against the blue of the sky, her shadow running below her, blotting out the sunlight. She hurled herself up, up, up until she was only a smudge on the blue-paper sky, and she circled in ever-widening circles, swooping and rising again, turning cartwheels in the sky.

They watched till she was gone, a speck of darkness disappearing beyond the trees.

Dobby closed his eyes and imagined he was the eagle in the air, flying with slow, strong wing-beats through the deep emptiness, floating on the updrafts, hurtling down, his body a feathered missile, braking so suddenly and so fiercely that smoke rose from his talons.

"Let's get the hawk," Timmer said quietly.

The hawk came to them in a flurry of wings when Timmer opened the door. They carried him to where they released the eagle and let him go.

He found a low tree branch and perched, balancing himself on it, his weight making him sway as if he were blown by a strong wind.

Timmer and Dobby moved back and waited. Crickets cried from the dry stalks, and once Dobby saw the green flash of grasshopper wings. Timmer pulled off the long glove, and threw it on the ground beside him. He wiped sweat from his hand and arm on his shirt.

The hawk crouched, waiting with infinite patience. Now and then his head jerked, following a shadow, a small sound from the ground below him. A squirrel ran across the clearing, bustled up a scaly tree trunk while the hawk watched but made no move.

Dobby heard the grumble of his own stomach. He placed his folded hands over it and looked up at Timmer, but Timmer was watching the hawk.

It had been a long time since the apples. Dobby thought longingly of last night's chili, the bowls heaped high and steaming. His stomach grumbled again. Shut up, stomach! Wait, can't you?

Evening was beginning to creep around them when he heard Timmer draw in a soft breath. Dobby glanced up at him, then at the hawk. The reddish fantail was spread and the wings were slowly opening and closing.

"He's going," Timmer whispered. The bird rose and hung motionless in the air. Then it plummeted down, straight for them, and Dobby heard the whine of the wind through the hawk's wings. He raised an arm to ward it off, but the hawk swooped past him, hovering over Timmer, its talons flexed, ready to grip.

"Reach me the glove, fast," Timmer said quietly.

Dobby darted forward. He got the long glove into Timmer's hand, but Timmer had no time to pull it on. The hawk dropped onto his left arm. Dobby saw the talons close and lock over Timmer's shirt sleeve, and he saw Timmer's face turn a strange gray color and his eyes half close with pain. The glove dangled from his right hand. Dobby tugged his shirt free of his waist and flapped it nervously at the hawk. "Shoo! Get away!"

Timmer's voice was low, so low that it seemed far away. "Dobby. Come up on us quietly. Don't frighten him or he'll start bating. Help me get the glove on."

Dobby swallowed. The hawk was watching him. Through the torn sleeve of Timmer's shirt he could see where the flesh was open, the blood trickling down to Timmer's hand, the blue of the

shirt turning black from elbow to cuff. He was frightened.

"*Kee-yelp,*" the hawk screamed. Its talons flexed on Timmer's arm, and Timmer's neck muscles tightened.

Dobby moved slowly and cautiously. Timmer held out his right arm, and Dobby took the glove and worked it up and over Timmer's hand. The hawk cocked its head, watching curiously.

He heard Timmer talking to the bird, murmuring soft things that had no meaning, and sweat ran down Dobby's face as he slid the glove up and over Timmer's elbow.

"Get in the jeep, Dobby. Leave us alone."

Dobby backed away. Blood dropped to the ground between Timmer's feet, each drop making a little soft sucking noise as it hit the dirt. Dobby ran, hearing his breath coming in great sobbing gulps.

The jeep was warm from the heat of the day. He sat on the edge of the seat, staring through the window, and he saw Timmer lift his foot and rest it on a fallen tree, laying the arm that held the hawk's weight across his bent knee. His lips still moved, saying words that Dobby couldn't hear. Slowly, slowly, he brought his other arm forward, holding his gloved fist under the hawk's breast.

The talons opened and with an awkward flap of his wings, the hawk took his stand on Timmer's fist.

Timmer's left arm dropped to his side, the shirt sleeve hanging in tatters, and Dobby saw the bright red gashes where the hawk had been. A wave of sickness washed over him.

Then he saw Timmer's bloodied hand come up and gently rub the hawk's head. Timmer was murmuring, smiling. The hawk allowed himself to be petted. And clear, clear as though he looked through binoculars, Dobby saw Timmer's face. There was no fear there, no hate. There was nothing but gentleness. Dobby clenched his fists. Something stirred in him, a kind of melting softness that he couldn't understand, and he wished, he wished that Timmer would look that way at him.

He saw Timmer's arm dart up, launching the hawk into the valley below. Dobby threw the jeep door open and ran, stumbling and gasping across the space between them.

Timmer shaded his eyes with his gloved arm and watched the bird circling and circling below them. "Timmer," Dobby whispered, but Timmer stood still, his body straining skyward. The hawk rose, taking the wind, flying up now, up, up, until he was gone from sight in the darkening sky.

Timmer turned away. "It's called 'the point of pride,'" he said slowly. "The very highest point the bird can reach in flight." His voice was blurred and he stumbled as he turned.

Dobby picked up his shirt where he had dropped it. He shook off the dust and held it out. "Do you want to put this around your arm? It's a little dirty . . ."

"I'll be O.K." Timmer bent over, examining the long, deep gashes that circled his arm like crimson bracelets. "Miss Bee'll fix me up when we get home."

"Dumb bird," Dobby said. "What did he have to do that for?" He ran ahead to get the jeep door open for Timmer.

"It was my fault." Timmer pulled himself into the driver's seat. "He was looking for the glove and I'd taken it off." He closed his eyes for a second and leaned his head forward against the steering wheel.

"I wish I could drive," Dobby said. He was mad at himself for being so useless. And I was going to drive to China, he thought. Some chance. "Does it hurt bad?" he asked.

Timmer fished the keys from his pocket and turned on the ignition. "It hurts. But it's my own fault. *I* knew it was time for the hawk to go. How was he supposed to know?"

"Sometimes that happens at the Center, too," Dobby said slowly.

Maria McBride. She was nine or ten when she was placed in a foster home. It was her first placement because she had all kinds of what they called disturbances that they had to help her with first. When her new family came for her, she hid in a closet.

Dobby remembered Maria standing in the hallway, crying and clinging to Mrs. Pruitt as if she'd never let her go. Mrs. Pruitt had to pry Maria's arms off and sort of push her away. It was really weird. Afterward Mrs. Pruitt's eyes had that misty look again and she said, "She's going to be all right. Maria's going to be all right." Thinking about it now, Dobby figured Mrs. Pruitt had been maybe saying it to herself.

"Sometimes *they* think they're ready and I know they're not," Timmer said. His words ran together, jumbled, but when Timmer turned to look at Dobby his eyes were clear.

The chill night air whistled past the jeep. Dobby shivered and pulled on his shirt. Grit rubbed against his skin. What a miserable rotten day this had turned out to be.

7

It was dark when they got back to the old barn. Miss Bee came out to meet them, carrying one of the lanterns. Rooster glared at them from the curve of her arm. His eyes glinted in the lamplight.

Miss Bee clucked when she saw Timmer's wounds.

"And not a thing here to clean them with, I expect," she said crossly.

"Nothing but water." Timmer sounded weary.

"Well, you'll just have to come with me to my place. Did you get your tetanus booster that time I told you it was due?"

"I always do what you tell me." Timmer grinned a shaky grin, and Dobby saw that the arm he held out for Miss Bee's inspection trembled.

Miss Bee cocked her head to one side, considering. "The best thing's for the boy to stay here and you drive me and Rooster back in the jeep. I got bandages and things at the house. I think you could use a spot of my brandy, too, by the looks of you. Helps put the blood back." Timmer supported himself by bracing his good arm against the jeep. "Dobby can come with us," he said.

Miss Bee looked Dobby up and down, raising and lowering the lantern. "Nope. He'd better stay. Somebody's after your birds. He came all the way up the path today, thinking there was nobody here. Snuck along behind the bushes on his hands and knees. But I saw him. Me and Rooster came out after him and he took off back toward the road. I heard a car motor start up right after. He's a little runt of a fellow. Wears one of those short navy coats."

Dobby nibbled at his thumbnail. He didn't want to be left. What if somebody came when he was all alone? It would be hairy. But it *would* make up some to Timmer for the jeep and everything. He scuffed his feet in the dirt. "I'll stay."

"Well, I don't know," Timmer said.

Could somebody have a fuzzy voice, Dobby wondered. That's how Timmer sounded. Fuzzy and furry as though he talked through a mouthful of feathers.

Miss Bee looked Dobby over again. "He's kinda

runty himself," she said at last, "and he doesn't look like he's got much muscle, but still and all . . ."

Dobby glared. Silly old bat. "I'm just as big as you," he said. "And my muscles are big. They're the kind that don't show." He clenched his fists, hoping for a bulge big as a football at the top of his arms, waiting for Miss Bee to call Timmer's attention to it.

"Why, look at that, Timmer! Look at that boy there! With muscles like that he could lift a tank. You'd better keep him here, Timmer. You can bet you won't find another boy with muscles like that!"

"He'd be better than nothing, Timmer," Miss Bee said. "Mind you stay out of sight, though." she told Dobby. "And if you hear anything, bang a few pans on the table or something and don't let him see you. Maybe he'll think it's me. He's real scared of me."

I bet, Dobby thought.

Timmer spoke in his slow slurred voice. "Can you hack it by yourself, Dobby?"

"We'll be back in a half hour, maybe less," Miss Bee added.

"I'll be O.K." Dobby tried to make it sound convincing.

"Get in then, Miss Bee," Timmer said. His arm hung by his side like it didn't belong to him.

"I got the alarm rope up," Miss Bee said, settling herself in the jeep and handing the lantern through the window to Dobby. The lantern light made her rings wink and twinkle. "Mind you don't trip over it."

Dobby hoped she could see his "drop dead" look in the lamplight. He gave a little sniff to let her know what he thought of her, in case her eyes weren't too good, then a louder snort in case her ears weren't too good either.

"Wait a second." Miss Bee took the whistle from around her neck. "If you hear anything, blow. There's nothing a thief's more afraid of than a whistle. And on a clear night like this we'll hear you across the field at my place."

Dobby spun the whistle in his hand.

"You sure?" Timmer asked.

Dobby nodded.

"I'll send back some duck eggs for your supper," Miss Bee called. "Felicity is laying well."

Dobby held the lantern high and watched the red taillights bump up and down till they disappeared into the darkness.

It was very still, so still that he could hear his own thoughts scurrying around in the little tunnels of his brain. Doing it for Timmer! What did he care about Timmer? Nothing, that's what. He could run away again. No, he couldn't run away again.

"Oh, rats!" he snapped out loud. His words

sounded small and timid in the night silence. He strung the whistle around his neck, walked to the side of the barn, and jumped the alarm rope. See, he told the night. I'm not scared. Nothin' to be scared of.

But still, it was good to get inside, out of the empty dark.

The Cooper's hawk clawed at its wire the way an old stray cat had scratched at the window of the Center one rainy night. Dobby took the lantern and went hesitantly across to the corner.

"Hello," he said. The hawk watched him as carefully as he watched it. "I know I don't *like* you," Dobby said, "so what am I hanging around here for?"

The hawk picked at its belly with its beak. How could Timmer like these dumb hawks and eagles, Dobby wondered? What was it that made him stay here, day after day, training them only to let them go?

He prowled around the barn. There was a piece of hard cheese in the refrigerator, and he ate it in three bites. None of the books on the shelf looked interesting. *The Vanishing Eagle, Common Diseases of American Birds, Bird of Jove*. Not even a *National Geographic* or a *Sports Illustrated*. He took *The Vanishing Eagle* over to the table and began to leaf through it, longing for the sound of the jeep to come back, for the good reassuring thump of the engine.

Dobby came to a picture of an eagle crouched over its food, wings spread as though hiding its kill from anyone wanting to steal it. The picture reminded Dobby of the way Karl Miller hunched over his plate when they had spaghetti for dinner. In big letters under the picture it said, "EAGLE MANTLING ITS FOOD." Dobby grinned. The next time Karl Miller did that he'd tell him to stop mantling. The next time! But he'd be in Juvie! A shiver crept along his arms and ran up his neck.

Did he imagine it, or was it very, very quiet now, as though the barn held its breath, listening? Dobby held his breath, too. The darkness outside seemed to press against the walls, and he turned his head slowly to examine the closed door and the high window. Where was Timmer? Wasn't it time he came back? In the corner the hawk moved uneasily.

There was a noise outside. Dobby gripped the edge of the book so hard that he saw his knuckles turn patchy pink. Every bit of him listened.

There it was again. A sort of scuffling and a clanking. From somewhere Dobby remembered a TV movie about Frankenstein, where the monster had come walking, stiff-legged, dragging a chain, his terrible eyes glaring, staring . . .

He jumped up. The lantern shook in his hand as he tiptoed over to the door. He pressed his ear against the rough wood, but all was quiet. He heard only the thick thump-thumping of his heart.

The sound came again. Then he heard a stifled sneeze. It was a person, not a monster, and the person was outside. He flung the door open and stumbled out.

For a second he could see nothing in the darkness, and he stopped, blinking blindly, hearing louder noises. The crunch, crunch of quick feet on the gravel path and the flap of wings. He moved his head slowly from side to side and his eyes focused again.

A man was running down the path, and the flashlight in his hand jumped up and down, sending its beam now into the trees, now across the field, lighting up the perches. The perches were empty—all empty!

"Yah!" the man shouted, "Yah!" He ran into the field where the birds stood free, their eyes shining like cats' eyes in the shaft of light.

Dobby was stunned. The man wasn't trying to *steal* the birds. He was setting them free!

"Yah! Yah! Fly, you dopes, fly!" the man screamed, rushing at the birds, flailing his arms, his voice harsh and croaking. Two of the birds rose clumsily, veering off into the darkness.

Dobby swallowed. He jumped down the steps. The birds! Timmer's birds! His fingers found the whistle on its long cord, and he blew and blew and blew and blew, sending the shrill scream into the air so loud that his ears and teeth ached from the sound.

The man turned. "It doesn't matter," he yelled. "You won't get in my way. Let the big one come and the old woman, too. They can't stop me now. It's too late."

Dobby began running along the path, scattering gravel, stumbling, getting himself up again. He blew the whistle again, then spat it from his mouth. "Go away!" he yelled. "What do you think you're doing!"

Now the field was a nightmare, filled with the dark moving bird bodies, their loud cries of fear and the feverish flapping of their wings. The man kept jabbing at them, urging them to fly. A Cooper's hawk lashed out with a flexed talon and tore a chunk from the man's pant leg, and the man brushed at the bird mindlessly as though it were a mosquito.

"Shoo! Go! You're free now. Go!" the man screamed. But the birds only shuffled out of his way adding their shrill cries to his. There was a smell in the air, the sickly sweet smell of the birds' terror. Dobby stepped back as the man turned and charged down the path. The man's face was wild and scary, wilder than the birds. Dobby took another step back, but the man kept coming and coming.

"Leave the birds alone!" Dobby shrieked. He saw the man pick up a piece of broken timber and run back to the birds, waving it like a club.

Dobby dropped the lantern. He flung himself

forward, aiming for the back of the man's legs, and he crashed against their bony hardness. The man fell, and Dobby scrabbled to hold onto the legs that kicked in and out like scissors.

"Leave the birds alone. They're Timmer's birds." His voice was muffled against the man's dark jacket that smelled of cigarettes smoked a long time ago. The slitted light from the lantern made shadows of the trees and the birds and of the two of them struggling on the gravel. One of the birds came closer, shaped like a vulture in the half darkness.

"It's wrong. They should be free!" The man gasped. And he was up again, first on his knees and then on his feet. But Dobby held on. Dobby was dragged along the path. The gravel, like broken glass, peeled the skin from the side of his face. Birds circled around them, and one hawk kept diving, screeching its anger. The man swiped at the air around it, driving it away.

"Stupid! Stupid!" Dobby wailed. "They'll die. It's not time for them to go. They're not ready to be free." He was astonished by his own words. He wondered at the truth of them—that he saw the truth so clearly.

He couldn't hold on any longer. Every bit of him ached. His hands were on fire. His cheek was raw. Pieces of gravel had worked their way inside his shirt and he could feel them sharp as needles. He let go and lay there on the path, hurting every-where.

The man stepped across him and Dobby made one last weak effort to grab the foot in the heavy boot. The foot came back and Dobby felt a dull blow on the side of his head. Spots, like shiny black raisins, swirled inside his mind. And there were words swirling, too, words that were lit up like the signs on movie houses.

"BOY! BOY! I DIDN'T MEAN TO HURT YOU. I DIDN'T MEAN TO HURT YOU."

He opened his eyes. How heavy his eyes were! How could eyes be heavy? Through the dancing raisins he saw the man's face, a blurry face that bent over him.

Then the strangest thing happened. The man turned into a gigantic eagle, big as a house, and the eagle began opening its wings, slowly, powerfully. The wings blotted out the field and the barn and the trees and the sky. "What you're doing is called mantling," Dobby told the bird. He figured he hadn't said the words out loud, though, because the eagle didn't seem to hear him.

He opened his eyes wide, and the bird disappeared. Instead there was the man face again, very small, getting smaller and smaller. He'd imagined the bird. "Got to stop this imagining," he said. "Going to stop it." But if he had imagined the bird why were the wings still closing in on him, covering him, shutting him inside their warm soft darkness?

8

Dobby lay with his eyes shut, listening to the voices. There was always talking in the rooms at night, especially when you were trying to sleep, though usually Mrs. Pruitt or Hazeline would come in and tell everyone to keep quiet. But these voices were different and they didn't belong to anyone he knew.

"You mean it was one of the Jacobs' boys from over on Elm Street?" a woman asked. "Sam Jacobs' son?"

"It was Frank, the youngest one," a soft girl voice said. "I know him because he's been down to OPC a few times."

"Huh!" Dobby heard a sniff. "He's not all that

101

young," the first woman said. "He's thirty if he's a day. He's the one was the navy flier."

"He was shot down over Vietnam and spent a year in a prison camp," the girl voice said.

"Sure. I remember now." That was the woman again. "Didn't he go down and stand outside the county jail holding signs about freeing the prisoners? Wanted them all to be let out on the streets again?"

"Yes, he did." The girl voice was sad. "Poor guy. I'll have to try to get him some help through the VA."

"He had Dobby's head on his lap when we got there," Timmer said. "He kept muttering that he didn't mean to hurt him."

Timmer! Timmer's voice. Dobby remembered.

He opened his eyes and saw that he was lying in the sleeping bag. The big, raftered barn roof spread above him like a tent, and the window square was bright with moonlight. Slowly, cautiously, he moved his head and pain zigzagged up the back, across the top, and down his nose. He raised his hand and found a bump as big as a chestnut behind his ear. Everything ached.

"What happened here?" he whispered. At the sound of his voice all other noise ceased.

"Dobby!" Timmer pushed his chair back from the table and ran over to the sleeping bag. To Dobby he was so tall he might as well have been on stilts. His left arm was bandaged from wrist to

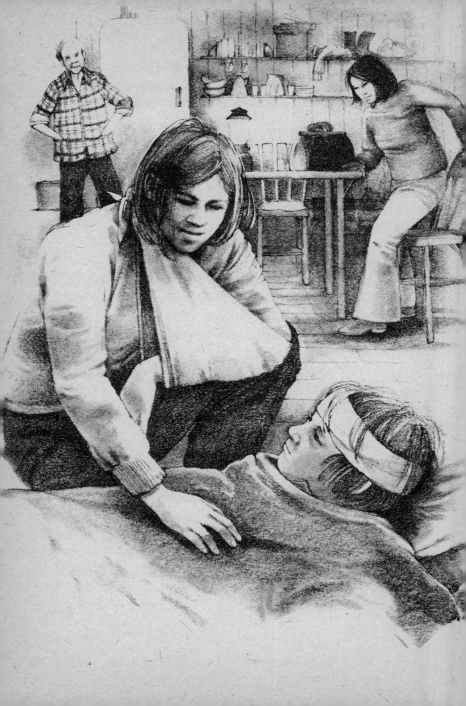

elbow, and a red scarf sling hung empty around his neck. He knelt down. "How do you feel?"

"O.K. I guess." He had other things to say, but words hurt. "You . . . you're not disappointed any more? You'd leave the keys?"

For a second Timmer looked at him blankly, not understanding. Then he smiled. "I'd leave the keys." There was a gentleness in his face that Dobby remembered seeing somewhere before.

Two women came up behind him, and Dobby saw that one woman was Miss Bee, still in her turned-up jeans and yellow boots, and that the other was little and thin. Her hair was long and straight and black as licorice. She carried a small leather bag.

"Can you move back, Timmer, and let me see him?" she asked firmly.

Dobby put out his hand and touched Timmer's leg. "The birds?" he asked. "The man?"

"The man's gone," Timmer said. "And I don't think he'll be back. He couldn't understand why the birds wouldn't fly away. I tried to explain it to him, to tell him they have things to learn before they go. But I don't think he understood."

Dobby wet his lips. "*I* understand." He closed his eyes for a second and when he opened them he saw Timmer's face, very serious.

"You do?" Timmer asked.

"Yes. But the birds didn't go. I thought they'd go when they had the chance."

"Nope. Someone brought in a pile of road kill while we were gone. Miss Bee had fed them all to save us doing it in the morning since we have to go to Glendon. They were full, and it was night, and they're used to it here." He grinned. "There's a red-tail missing, but I have a feeling she's up in the eucalyptus and that she'll be back down in the morning."

Dobby closed his eyes again. It had all been for nothing then. The fear, the fight, the hurting and holding on. All for nothing.

"The problem was," Timmer said, and it was as though he read Dobby's mind, "the Jacobs guy was so busy trying to free them that he would have injured them, really hurt them bad. A crippled bird is not free. I had a hard time making him understand that, too."

The young woman with the licorice hair touched Timmer's arm and he moved aside. "My turn," she said. "Hello, Dobby. I'm Dr. Chang."

"You're a doctor?" Dobby whispered.

She smiled warmly. "I sure am. And I understand *you* are a brave boy." She knelt down and took a stethoscope out of the leather bag.

Dobby heard Miss Bee say, "Come and finish your eggs, Timmer, before they get cold. When I fix Felicity's eggs, I like to see a body enjoy them."

Dr. Chang poked and prodded. Her fingers were long and thin and strong enough to hurt when they found a sore spot. Dobby was glad when she stopped and stood up.

"I think he's going to be all right, Miss Bee. But I'd like to get some X rays tomorrow. Maybe he could come down to OPC."

"OPC?" Dobby whispered.

For a second the long fingers brushed his hair and he saw her smile. "Out-Patient Clinic. Nothing to worry about."

Miss Bee nodded. "I'll call Emily Pruitt and tell her as soon as I get back to the house. Something else I want to ask her anyways."

Timmer lifted Dobby's head and helped him drink some grape juice. "You sure look a mess," he said. "Mrs. Pruitt's going to think my nice gentle birds clawed you."

"Well, one sure clawed you," Dobby whispered, and Timmer grinned.

Dr. Chang pulled down her sweater sleeves. "This is some crazy hospital you're running, Timmer," she said cheerfully. "One case of concussion, one lacerated arm, and a hawk with an amputated leg." ——

Timmer lowered Dobby's head gently onto the sleeping bag and stood up. "Thanks for coming, Doctor Chang," he said. "I didn't know if you made barn calls. Miss Bee said she was sure you did."

Dr. Chang smiled. "I have to admit it's the first one!"

106

Miss Bee rattled bowls on the table. "Leave these for Steve to do in the morning, Timmer. We don't want to get that bandage wet." She took a pink wicker basket, big as a suitcase, off one of the packing cases. "If you can give me a ride back to the house, doctor, it'll save Timmer's going out." She came across and stood over Dobby. All of the rings on all of her fingers shot off sparks bright enough to make Dobby's eyes ache.

"I've left three of Felicity's eggs for your breakfast. Make sure you eat them. Felicity lays the healthiest eggs in Ventura County." Her head poked forward. "You sure are spunky for a kid with no muscles." She stood for so long looking down at him that Dobby began to feel real jumpy. He wished he could slide his head down under the sleeping bag, but it hurt too much even thinking about it.

"Where's Rooster?" he whispered. Moving his lips made the bump hurt, but it was worse to just lie there and be looked at.

"He was sleeping, so I snuck out. He doesn't like to be left, even though Felicity's there and Henrietta and Tom Turkey." She sighed. "I've got all kinds of birds, but I've spoiled him, I guess. He's my favorite." She hitched the basket over her arm. "Well, so long, Dobby. I hope I'll see you again."

"Bye," Doctor Chang said. Dobby heard the barn door swing open, and he felt the cool night air drift in and puff against his face. The lantern shivered. Car doors slammed and an engine started. The Cooper's hawk settled itself noisily in the corner, and over its shuffling he heard Timmer's footsteps crunching back.

"You asleep, Dobby?" ·

"No."

Timmer sat cross-legged on his own sleeping bag and eased his arm gently into the sling.

"I'm sorry you got hurt, Dobby. And thank you for taking care of the birds."

Dobby nodded. A small hammer tap-tapped at the side of his skull.

"It was my fault," Timmer went on. "I stayed too long at Miss Bee's. I was just ready to go when we heard the whistle."

The tick of the clock was extra loud.

"You have to go back to the Center, Dobby. You know that."

"Yeah."

"Do you think . . . if I asked them they'd let you come out here sometimes to help Steve and me with the birds?"

"I don't know."

"Miss Bee's going to ask, too."

"They said they'd send me to Juvenile Hall next time I ran away."

"Oh." Timmer stood up quickly and began to undress, one-handed. "Well, Doctor Chang says they might figure coming here would be acceptable therapy or something like that. They might go for it."

"Could be. That's the kind of crap they do go for at the Center." Dobby raised a slow arm to cover his eyes. He didn't want to go back. He didn't want to go back.

"I won't run away again anyway," he said unsteadily. "I know that."

Timmer looked at him for a moment, then bent to turn out the lantern. Dobby heard the soft rustling as Timmer eased himself into the sleeping bag.

"Freedom's funny," Timmer's voice was warm in the dark. "It's the right of every creature who knows how to use it. I can teach the birds. People need to learn, too."

"Yeah," Dobby said. "I know."

Dobby closed his eyes. And there again was the eagle flying with slow strong wingbeats through the endless blue of the sky.

Someday, Dobby promised himself. Someday.

The MS READ-a-thon needs young readers!

Boys and girls between 6 and 14 can join the MS READ-a-thon and help find a cure for Multiple Sclerosis by reading books. And they get two rewards — the enjoyment of reading, and the great feeling that comes from helping others.

Parents and educators: For complete information call your local MS chapter, or call toll-free (800) 243-6000. Or mail the coupon below.

Kids can help, too!

- - - - - - - - - - - - - - -

Mail to:
National Multiple Sclerosis Society
205 East 42nd Street
New York, N.Y. 10017
I would like more information about the MS READ-a-thon and how it can work in my area.

Name _____
(please print)
Address _____
City _____ State _____ Zip _____
Organization _____

MS-10/77